Date: 6/17/14

J BIO DOUGLAS
Mattern, Joanne,
Marjory Stoneman Douglas /

D1709989

MARJORY STONEMAN DOUGLAS

JOANNE MATTERN

ABDO Publishing Company

visit us at
www.abdopublishing.com

Published by ABDO Publishing Company, PO Box 398166, Minneapolis, MN 55439.
Copyright © 2014 by Abdo Consulting Group, Inc. International copyrights reserved in all countries. No part of this book may be reproduced in any form without written permission from the publisher. The Checkerboard Library™ is a trademark and logo of ABDO Publishing Company.

Printed in the United States of America, North Mankato, Minnesota.
112013
012014

 PRINTED ON RECYCLED PAPER

Cover Photos: iStockphoto; The State Archives of Florida
Interior Photos: Alamy pp. 17, 29; AP Images p. 27; CARLTON WARD/National Geographic Creative pp. 21, 23; Corbis p. 19; Getty Images pp. 15, 24–25; iStockphoto pp. 1, 18; JIM ABERNETHY/National Geographic Creative p. 21; The State Archives of Florida pp. 5, 7, 9, 11, 13

Editors: Rochelle Baltzer, Tamara L. Britton, Bridget O'Brien
Art Direction: Neil Klinepier

Library of Congress Cataloging-in-Publication Data

Mattern, Joanne, 1963-
  Marjory Stoneman Douglas / Joanne Mattern.
      pages cm. -- (Conservationists)
  Includes index.
  ISBN 978-1-62403-093-2
1. Douglas, Marjory Stoneman--Juvenile literature. 2. Conservationists--Florida--Biography--Juvenile literature. 3. Everglades (Fla.)--Juvenile literature. I. Title.
  QH31.D645M38 2014
  333.72092--dc23
  [B]
                          2013029172

CONTENTS

LOVE OF NATURE

For many years, people thought of Florida's Everglades as a big swamp. But Marjory Stoneman Douglas knew that the Everglades was a special place. She helped people see that it was an important part of Florida's **ecosystem**.

Marjory Stoneman was born on April 7, 1890, in Minneapolis, Minnesota. Her father was Frank Bryant Stoneman. He was a businessman. Her mother, Florence Lillian Trefethen, was a violinist. Marjory was Frank and Lillian's only child.

Marjory was very close to her parents. They taught her to love nature. When she was a little girl, her father read a poem to her. The poem was "The Song of Hiawatha" by Henry Wadsworth Longfellow.

In the poem, Hiawatha carves the bark from a birch tree to make a canoe. When she heard that, Marjory cried. She was sad that the tree had to die so Hiawatha could have his canoe.

Marjory in 1894

YOUNG MARJORY

Marjory's father owned several businesses. But each eventually failed. The family moved often so he could start again. Frequently starting over was hard on Marjory's mother. Lillian and Frank argued a lot. This situation was stressful for Marjory.

When she was six years old, Marjory's parents divorced. Lillian and Marjory moved to Taunton, Massachusetts. There, they lived with Lillian's parents and sister Fanny.

Lillian's family was angry with Frank. They said bad things about him. But Marjory did not believe them. She learned to make up her own mind. Later, Marjory wrote, "To this day, I still don't believe everything people tell me."

Marjory loved school and enjoyed reading. She was good at every subject except math. Marjory had many girlfriends. However, she felt uneasy around boys. In high school, Marjory felt unpopular. "I was fat, my hair was greasy, I wore glasses, I giggled, I was completely self-conscious with boys."

Lillian Stoneman

College Days

After graduating from high school, Marjory wanted to go to college. But Lillian had many health problems. Marjory thought she should stay home and care for her mother.

However, Marjory's grandmother knew Marjory had to live her own life. She thought Marjory would be able to support herself if she became a teacher. She and Marjory's aunt Fanny had some money saved. They paid for Marjory to go to college.

In 1908, Marjory left home for Wellesley College near Boston, Massachusetts. All the students at Wellesley were women. Marjory was happy that she didn't have to worry about boys! At Wellesley, she learned to be herself.

Marjory loved college. Her favorite classes were English and **composition**. Marjory wrote stories that were published in the college **literary** magazine. She was very proud of herself.

When she was a senior, Marjory (front row, center) *got a jump start on her future literary career. She became the editor of* Legenda, *her college yearbook.*

One of Marjory's most interesting classes was **elocution**. In this class, students learn to speak clearly and correctly. Later, she would be very glad she had taken this course.

During Marjory's third year of college, Lillian became sick. She had to have an operation. Marjory spent her summer vacation taking care of her mother.

STARTING OUT

In June 1912, Marjory graduated from Wellesley. It was a happy day for her. But later that day, her aunt Fanny gave her some terrible news. Marjory's mother had breast **cancer**. Marjory rushed home. When Lillian died a few weeks later, Marjory was at her side.

Marjory was at a turning point in her life. She missed her mother very much. She also had to decide what kind of work she would do. Her grandmother still wanted her to be a teacher. But Marjory did not want to teach.

Marjory took a job in a department store. But she was unhappy with the work. Then she met Kenneth Douglas. He was the editor of the *Newark Evening News*. He was 30 years older than she was, but he asked her on a date. Three months later, they were married.

Soon afterward, Kenneth went to prison. He had stolen money. He also had tried to steal money from Frank Stoneman.

Marjory's uncle came to visit her. He told her that her husband was nothing but trouble. He also said that her father wanted to see her. Frank Stoneman had a new wife and a new home in Florida. He invited Marjory to live with them. Marjory said yes. She divorced Kenneth and prepared to move to Florida.

After she married, Marjory was able to quit her department store job. She then cared for the couple's home.

FLORIDA

Douglas left for Florida in September of 1915. She was 25 years old. She had not seen her father for almost 20 years! She was excited and scared.

But Douglas should not have worried. When she met her father at the Miami train station they kissed and hugged. Then they went home and met Douglas's stepmother, Lilla. Douglas and Lilla became good friends.

Douglas's father ran a newspaper called the *Miami Herald*. He asked Douglas to work for him as a reporter. Douglas loved the job. "Suddenly, I found what I was meant to do. I didn't care what I was writing about as long as it was writing," she explained.

Douglas wrote hundreds of articles. She wrote about the people who lived in Miami. She wrote about their problems and adventures. At that time, Miami was not a big city. South Florida was wild and undeveloped. Much of the land was wilderness.

Frank Stoneman was the Miami Herald's editor in chief from 1910 to 1941.

SERVING PEOPLE

In 1916, much of the world was fighting **World War I**. To do her part, Douglas joined the American Red Cross in 1918. She went to Paris, France. There, she helped people who had lost everything in the war.

In 1920, Douglas came home. She continued to work at the *Miami Herald*. She also continued her public service. She helped poor African Americans who lived in Miami. Many lived in houses that had no bathrooms or running water. These unhealthy conditions poisoned the community's water.

Douglas wrote articles describing how difficult it was for the people to stay healthy. Because of her work, a law was passed. It said every house in Miami had to have an indoor bathroom. Douglas also set up a program to lend money to families so they could install running water in their homes.

By 1924, Douglas was tired. She worked so hard serving her community and at her newspaper that she could not sleep. Finally, Douglas had to leave her job at the newspaper.

Today, Douglas's house is on the United States' National Register of Historic Places.

Douglas become a **freelance** writer. Her stories and articles were published in magazines. In 1926, she had enough money to build a house of her own in Miami's Coconut Grove neighborhood. It was one big room, with a small kitchen and bedroom. Douglas loved her house because it was simple and open to nature.

FUN FACT:

Before joining the Red Cross, Douglas served for a year in the US Naval Reserve.

SERVING THE ENVIRONMENT

Douglas enjoyed spending time in the Everglades. The Everglades was an area of water and tall plants called saw grass. There, Douglas watched thousands of birds fly over her head. She fell in love with this strange, beautiful place.

In 1942, a man named Hervey Allen came to Douglas's house to visit. Allen worked for a publishing company called Rinehart & Co. The company was producing a series of books called Rivers of America. Allen asked Douglas to write a book about the Miami River.

In researching the Miami River, Douglas found it began in the Everglades. She learned the Everglades itself was a slow-moving river. She asked Allen if she could write about the Everglades. Allen said yes. "I was hooked with the idea that would consume me for the rest of my life," Douglas later said.

Douglas once said the Miami River was only "about an inch long." It is actually 5.5 miles (9 km) long. It begins in the Everglades and runs through downtown Miami on its way to Biscayne Bay.

THE RIVER OF GRASS

Douglas set out to learn everything she could about the Everglades. The research would take more than three years. Douglas learned that the Everglades begins at Lake Okeechobee. From there,

The Everglades provides a home for 350 documented species of birds.

the water flows south to Florida Bay and the Gulf of Mexico.

Many people thought the Everglades was just a swamp. But Douglas found that it had fresh running water, like a river. The water was surrounded by saw grass. Douglas called the Everglades a "river of grass."

CONSERVATION ALERT!
The original Everglades stretched all the way from Orlando, Florida, to Florida Bay.

18

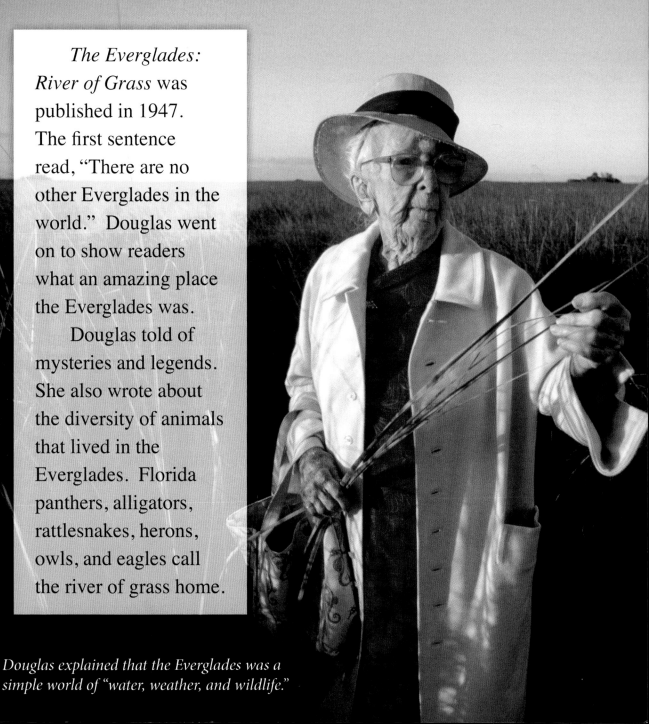

The Everglades: River of Grass was published in 1947. The first sentence read, "There are no other Everglades in the world." Douglas went on to show readers what an amazing place the Everglades was.

Douglas told of mysteries and legends. She also wrote about the diversity of animals that lived in the Everglades. Florida panthers, alligators, rattlesnakes, herons, owls, and eagles call the river of grass home.

Douglas explained that the Everglades was a simple world of "water, weather, and wildlife."

River in Trouble

Many people did not agree with Douglas. They wanted to drain the Everglades for sugar farming. Some wanted to erect dams to hold back the water and control flooding around Lake Okeechobee. Then farms, houses, and towns could be built there.

Douglas knew this was a terrible idea. Her book showed that if the Everglades were destroyed, south Florida would be hurt, too. In 1947, President Harry Truman **dedicated** the Everglades National Park. However, the park only protected a small portion of the Everglades. Much of the river of grass was still endangered.

Over the next 20 years, the government built canals and dams in the Everglades. The Army Corps of Engineers changed the course of the Kissimmee River, turning it into a canal. Because of these changes, less water flowed into the Everglades. The saw grass dried out. Chemicals from the towns and farms polluted the water. Many animals died.

The Everglades is home to 21 federally threatened and endangered species. These include the Florida panther and the loggerhead turtle.

Then in 1969, construction of the Everglades Jetport began in Big Cypress Swamp. Big Cypress Swamp bordered the Everglades. It supplied about one-third of the Everglades' water. If the airport were built, the Everglades and Big Cypress Swamp would both be in trouble.

FRIENDS FOREVER

Douglas believed the Everglades should be saved. So in 1969, she started Friends of the Everglades. She traveled all over Florida, and told people how important it was to protect the Everglades. Slowly, people began to listen.

In 1970, construction on the Everglades Jetport was abandoned. Four years later, President Gerald Ford signed a law that created Big Cypress National Preserve. The state of Florida passed laws to return the Kissimmee River to its natural state. New laws stopped the draining of water and construction in the Everglades. Gradually, the Everglades came back to life.

United States

N

FLORIDA

Atlantic Ocean

Kissimmee River

Lake Okeechobee

The Everglades

Miami

Gulf of Mexico

Everglades National Park

Florida Bay

In the 1960s, the US Army Corps of Engineers dredged and straightened the Kissimmee River. It was known as the C-38 Canal.

The Kissimmee River Restoration Project returned the river to its natural state. The project is expected to be complete by 2015.

FOLLOWING THROUGH

Friends of the Everglades and supporters of the **environment** were happy with what they had achieved. But there was more work to do to protect the Everglades.

In 1989, President George H.W. Bush signed the Everglades National Park Protection and Expansion Act. This law added more land to Everglades National

Lake Okeechobee is Florida's largest freshwater lake. Its name means "big water" in the Seminole Native American language.

Park. And, it created the park's Marjory Stoneman Douglas Visitor's Center.

In 1991, the Marjory Stoneman Douglas Everglades Protection Act became law. It provided money to restore the Everglades and the area's **ecosystems**.

Three years later, the Everglades Forever Act placed strict limits on the content of water runoff that was discharged into the Everglades. This stopped toxic substances from farms

and industries from being released into the Everglades.

In 2000, the Lake Okeechobee Protection Act passed. This law was designed to restore and protect the lake. It also paid to clean up pollution in the lake's **watershed**.

HIGH HONORS

Douglas's work had done much to preserve the Everglades. For this, she has received many awards. In 1975, the Florida Audubon Society named Douglas its Conservationist of the Year. In 1976, the Florida Wildlife Federation gave her the same honor.

In 1986, the National Parks Conservation Association created the Marjory Stoneman Douglas Award. It honors people who fight to protect the national park system.

In 1993, President Bill Clinton awarded Douglas the Presidential Medal of Freedom. This is the highest honor a U.S. **civilian** can receive. Douglas enjoyed receiving awards, but educating people to value the **environment** was the best reward of all.

FUN FACT:
In 2000, Douglas was named to the National Women's Hall of Fame.

On May 14, 1998, Marjory Stoneman Douglas died. She was 108 years old. In her long life, Douglas worked tirelessly to save the Everglades. Today, she is an inspiration to new generations of **environmentalists**. Because of her work, our only Everglades is preserved for future generations to enjoy.

Douglas talks with President Clinton after receiving her award.

TIMELINE

1890 Marjory Stoneman Douglas was born on April 7 in Minneapolis, Minnesota.

1912 Douglas graduated from Wellesley College; her mother Lillian Stoneman died.

1913 Douglas married Kenneth Douglas.

1915 Douglas divorced and moved to Miami, Florida.

1917 Douglas joined the US Naval Reserve.

1918 Douglas joined the American Red Cross.

1926 Douglas's home in the Coconut Grove area of Miami was completed.

1947 *The Everglades: River of Grass* was published; Everglades National Park was established.

1969 Douglas founded Friends of the Everglades.

1993 President Bill Clinton awarded Douglas the Presidential Medal of Freedom.

1998 On May 14, Marjory Stoneman Douglas died at age 108.

This visitor center is dedicated to the memory of

Ernest F. Coe

1866 - 1951

"Father of Everglades National Park"

United States Department of the Interior
National Park Service
Everglades National Park
Dedicated: December 6, 1996

ERNEST F. COE

Everglades National Park exists largely due to the efforts of Ernest F. "Tom" Coe.

In 1928, Coe formed the Tropical Everglades National Park Association. Marjory Stoneman Douglas was a member. Coe worked with the National Park Service and the state of Florida to establish the park.

On May 30, 1934, President Franklin D. Roosevelt signed an act to create the park. It took the next 13 years to acquire the land.

Because of his efforts, Coe is known as the Father of Everglades National Park.

"Whoever wants me to talk, I'll come over and tell them about the necessity of preserving the Everglades." —Marjory Stoneman Douglas

GLOSSARY

cancer - any of a group of often deadly diseases marked by harmful changes in the normal growth of cells. Cancer can spread and destroy healthy tissues and organs.

civilian - a person who is not an active member of the military.

composition - a type of writing, especially referring to brief essays.

dedicate - to open to public use.

ecosystem - a community of organisms and their surroundings.

elocution - the study of how to speak clearly and in a way that is effective and socially acceptable.

environmentalist - a person concerned with problems of the environment. The environment is all the surroundings that affect the growth and well-being of a living thing.

freelance - earning money by being hired to work on different jobs for short periods of time.

literary - of or relating to books or literature.

watershed - the area of land that includes a particular river or lake, and all the waterways that flow into it.

World War I - from 1914 to 1918, fought in Europe. Great Britain, France, Russia, the United States, and their allies were on one side. Germany, Austria-Hungary, and their allies were on the other side.

WEB SITES

To learn more about Marjory Stoneman Douglas, visit ABDO Publishing Company online. Web sites about Marjory Stoneman Douglas are featured on our Book Links page. These links are routinely monitored and updated to provide the most current information available.

www.abdopublishing.com

Index